HELPFULLY YOURS

Start Publishing PD LLC

Manufactured in the United States of America

Cover art: Shutterstock/Taisiya Kozorez

Cover design: Jennifer Do

10 9 8 7 6 5 4 3 2 1

ISBN 979-8-8809-0540-9

HELPFULLY YOURS

by Evelyn E. Smith

"Come down to Earth—and stay there!" is a humiliating order for somebody with wings! When in Rome do as the romans do . . . well unless you fly.

Tarb Morfatch had read all the information on Terrestrial customs that was available in the *Times* morgue before she'd left Fizbus. And all through the journey she'd studied her *Brief Introduction to Terrestrial Manners and Mores* avidly. Perhaps it was a bit overinspirational in spots, but it had facts in it, too.

So she knew that, since the natives were non-alate, she was not to take wing on Earth. She had, however, forgotten to correlate the knowledge of their winglessness with her own vertical habits. As a result, on leaving the tender that had ferried her down from the Moon, she looked up instead of right and narrowly escaped death at the jaws of a raging groundcar that swerved out onto the field.

She recognized it as a taxi from one of the pictures in the handbook. It was a pity, she thought sadly as she was knocked off her feet, that all those lessons she had so carefully learned were to go to waste.

But it was only the wind of the car's passage that had thrown her down. As she struggled to get up, hampered by her awkward native skirts, the door of the taxi flew open. A tall young man—a Fizbian—burst out, the soft yellowish-green down on his handsome face bristling with fright until each feather stood out separately.

"Miss Morfatch! Are you all right?"

"Just—just a little shaky," she murmured, brushing dirt from her rosy leg feathers. *Too young to be Drosmig; too good-looking to be anyone important, she thought glumly. Must be the office boy.*

To her surprise, he didn't help her up. Probably it would violate some native taboo if he did, she deduced. The handbook hadn't mentioned anything that seemed to apply, but, after all, a little book like that couldn't cover everything.

HELPFULLY YOURS

*

She could see the young man was embarrassed—his emerald crest was waving to and fro.

"I'm Stet Zarnon," he introduced himself awkwardly.

The Managing Editor! The handsome young employer of her girlish dreams! But perhaps he had a wife on Fizbus—no, the Grand Editor made a point of hiring people without families to use as a pretext for expensive vacations on the Home Planet.

As she opened her mouth to say something brilliantly witty, to show she was no ordinary female but a creature of spirit and fire and intelligence, a sudden cacophony of shrill cries and explosions arose, accompanied by bursts of light. Her feathers stood erect and she clung to her employer with both feathered legs.

"If these are the friendly diplomatic relations Earth and Fizbus are supposed to be enjoying," she said, "I'm not enjoying them one bit!"

"They're only taking pictures of you with native equipment," he explained, pulling away from her. What was the matter with him? "You're the first Fizbian woman ever to come to Terra, you know."

She certainly did know—and, what was more, she had made the semi-finals for Miss Fizbus only the year before. Perhaps he had some Terrestrial malady he didn't want her to catch. Or could it be that in the four years he had spent in voluntary exile on this planet, he had come to prefer the native females? Now it was her turn to shrink from him.

He was conversing rapidly in Terran with the chattering natives who milled about them. Although Tarb had been an honors student in Terran back at school, she found herself unable to understand more than an occasional word of what they said. Then she remembered that they were not at the world capital, Ottawa, but another community, New York. Undoubtedly they were all speaking some provincial dialect peculiar to the locality.

And nobody at all booed in appreciation, although, she told herself sternly, she really couldn't have expected them to. Standards of beauty were different in different solar systems. At least they were picking up as souvenirs some of the feathers she'd shed in her tumble, which showed they took an interest.

Stet turned back to her. "These are fellow-members of the press."

She was able to catch enough of what he said next in Terran to understand that she was being formally introduced to the aboriginal journalists. Although you could never call the natives attractive, with their squat figures and curiously atrophied vestigial wings—*arms*, she reminded herself—they were very Fizboid in appearance and, with their winglessness cloaked, could have creditably passed for singed Fizbians.

Moreover, they seemed friendly; at any rate, the sounds they uttered were welcoming. She began to make the three ritual *entrechats*, but Stat stopped her. "Just smile at them; that'll be enough."

It didn't seem like enough, but he was the boss.

*

"Thank the stars we're through with that," he sighed, as they finally were able to escape their confrères and get into the taxi. "I suppose," he added, wriggling inside the clumsy Terrestrial jacket which, cut to fit over his wings, did nothing either to improve his figure or to make him look like a native, "it was as much of an ordeal for you as for me."

"Well, I am a little bewildered by it all," Tarb admitted, settling herself as comfortably as possible on the seat cushions.

"No, don't do that!" he cried. "Here people don't crouch on seats. They sit," he explained in a kindlier tone. "Like this."

"You mean I have to bend myself in that clumsy way?"

He nodded. "In public, at least."

"But it's so hard on the wings. I'm losing feathers foot over claw."

"Yes, but you could. . . . " He stopped. "Well, anyhow, remember we have to comply with local customs. You see, the Terrestrials have those things called arms instead of legs. That is, they have legs, but they use them only for walking."

She sighed. "I'd read about the arms, but I had no idea the natives would be so—so primitive as to actually use them."

"Considering they had no wings, it was very clever of them to make use of the vestigial appendages," he said hotly. "If you take their physical limitations into account, they've done a marvelous job with their little planet. They can't fly; they have very little sense of balance; their vision is exceedingly poor—yet, in spite of all that, they have achieved a quite remarkable degree of civilization." He gestured toward the horizontal building arrangements visible through the window. "Why, you could almost call those streets. As a matter of fact, the natives do."

At the moment, she could take an interest in Terrestrial civilization only as it affected her personally. "But I'll be able to relax in the office, won't I?"

"To a certain extent," he replied cautiously. "You see, we have to use a good deal of native help because—well, our facilities are limited. . . . "

"Oh," she said.

Then she remembered that she was on Terra at least partly to demonstrate the pluck of Fizbian femininity. Back on Fizbus, most of the *Times* executives had been dead set against having a woman sent out as Drosmig's assistant. But Grupe, the Grand Editor, had overruled them. "Time we broke with tradition," he had said. He'd felt she could do the job, and, by the stars, she would justify his faith in her!

"Sounds like rather a lark," she said hollowly.

Stet brightened. "That's the girl!" His eyes, she noticed, were emerald shading into turquoise, like his crest. "I certainly hope you'll like it here. Very wise of Grupe to send a woman instead of a man, after all. Women," he went on quickly, "are so much better at working up the human interest angle. And Drosmig is out of commission most of the time, so it's you who'll actually be in charge of 'Helpfully Yours.'"

She herself in charge of the column that had achieved interstellar fame in three short years! Basically, it had been designed to give guidance, advice and, if necessary, comfort to those Fizbians who found themselves living on Terra, for the Fizbus *Times* had stood for public service from time immemorial. As Grupe had put it, "We don't run this paper for ourselves, Tarb, but for our readers. And the same applies to our Terrestrial edition."

With the growing development of trade and cultural relations between the two planets, the Fizbians on Earth were an ever-increasing number. But they were not the only readers of "Helpfully Yours." Reprinted in the parent paper, it was read with edification and pleasure all over Fizbus. Everyone wanted to learn more about the ancient and other-worldly Terran culture.

The handbook, *A Brief Introduction to Terrestrial Manners and Mores*, owed much of its content to "Helpfully Yours." A grateful, almost fulsome, introductory note had said so. But the column truly deserved all the praise that had been lavished upon it by the handbook. How well she had studied the thoughtful letters that filled it and the excellent and well-reasoned advice—erring, if it erred at all, on the side of overtolerance—that had been given in return. Of course, on Earth, spiritual adjustment apparently was more important than the physical; you could tell that from the questions that were asked. A number of the letters had been reprinted in an appendix to the manual.

New York

Dear Senbot Drosmig:

When in contact with Terrestrial culture, I find myself constantly overawed and weighed down by the knowledge of my own inadequacy. I cannot seem to appreciate the local art forms as disseminated by the juke box, the comic strip, the tabloid.

How can I help myself toward a greater understanding?

Hopefully yours,

Gnurmis Plitt

*

Dear Mr. Plitt:

Remember, Orkv was not excavated in a week. It took the Terrestrials many centuries to develop their exquisite and esoteric art forms. How can you expect to comprehend them in a few short years? Expose yourself to their art. Work, study, meditate.

Understanding will come, I promise you.

Helpfully yours,

Senbot Drosmig

*

Paris

Dear Senbot Drosmig:

To think that I am enjoying the benefits of Terra while my wife and little ones are forced to remain on Fizbus makes my heart ache. Surely it is not fair that I should have so much and they so little. Imagine the inestimable advantage to the fledgling of even a short contact with Terrestrial culture!

Why cannot my loved ones come to join me so that we can share all these wonderful spiritual experiences and be enriched by them together?

Poignantly yours,

Tpooly N'Ox

*

Dear Mr. N'Ox:

After all, it has been only five years since Fizbian spaceships first came into contact with Terra. In keeping with our usual colonial policy—so inappropriate and anachronistic when applied to a well-developed civilization like Terra's—at first only males are allowed to go to the new world until it is made certain over a period of years that the planet is safe for mothers and future mothers of Fizbus.

But Stet Zarnon himself, the celebrated and capable editor of the Terran edition of *The Fizbus Times*, has taken up your cause, and I promise you that eventually your loved ones will be able to join you.

Meanwhile, work, study, meditate.

Helpfully yours,

Senbot Drosmig

*

Ottawa

Dear Senbot Drosmig:

Having just completed a two-year tour of duty on Earth as part of a diplomatic mission, I am regretfully leaving this fair planet. What books, what objects of art, what, in short, souvenirs shall I take back to Fizbus which will give our people some small idea of Earth's rich cultural heritage and, at the same time, serve as useful and appropriate gifts for my friends and relatives back Home?

Inquiringly yours,

Solgus Zagroot

*

Dear Mr. Zagroot:

Take back nothing but your memories. They will be your best souvenirs.

Out of context, any other mementos might convey little, if anything, of the true beauty and advanced spirituality of Terrestrial culture, and you might cheapen them were you to use them crassly as souvenirs. Furthermore, it is possible that you, in your ignorance, might unwittingly select some items that give a distorted and false idea of our extrafizbian friends.

The Fizbian-Earth Cultural Commission, sponsored by *The Fizbian Times*, in conjunction with the consulate, is preparing a vast program of cultural interchange. Leave it to them to do the great work, for you can be sure they will do it well.

And be sure to tell your fellow-laborers in the diplomatic vineyards that it is wiser not to send unapproved Terran souvenirs back Home. They might cause a fatal misunderstanding between the two worlds. Tell them to spend their time on Earth in working, studying and meditating, rather than shopping.

Helpfully yours,

Senbot Drosmig

*

And now she—Tarb Morfatch—herself was going to be the guiding spirit that brought enlightenment and uplift to countless thousands on Terra and millions on Fizbus. Her name wouldn't appear on the columns, but the reward of having helped should be enough. Besides, Drosmig was due to retire soon. If she proved herself competent, she would take over the column entirely and get the byline. Grupe had promised faithfully.

But what, she wondered, had put Drosmig "out of commission"?

The taxi drew up before a building with a vulgar number of floors showing above ground.

"Ah—before we—er—meet the others," Stet suggested, twitching his crest, "I was wondering whether you would care to—er—have dinner with me tonight?"

This roused Tarb from her speculations. "Oh, I'd love to!" *A date with the boss right away!*

Stet fumbled in his garments for appropriate tokens with which to pay the driver. "You—you're not engaged or anything back Home, Miss Morfatch?"

"Why, no," she said. "It so happens that I'm not."

"Splendid!" He made an abortive gesture with his leg, then let her get out of the taxi by herself. "It makes the natives stare," he explained abashedly.

"But why shouldn't they?" she asked, wondering whether to laugh or not. "How could they help but stare? We are different." *He must be joking.* She ventured a smile.

He smiled back, but made no reply.

The pavement was hard under her thinly covered soles. Now that walking looked as if it would present a problem, the ban on wing use loomed more threateningly. She had, of course, walked before—on wet days when her wings were waterlogged or in high winds or when she had surface business. However, the sidewalks on Fizbus were soft and resilient. Now she understood why the Terrestrials wore such crippling foot armor, but that didn't make her feel any better about it.

A box-shaped machine took the two Fizbians up to the twentieth story in twice the time it would have taken them to fly the same distance. Tarb supposed that the offices were in an attic instead of a basement because exchange difficulties forced the *Times* to such economy. She wondered ruefully whether her own expense account would also suffer.

But it was no time to worry about such sordid matters; most important right now was making a favorable impression on her co-workers. She did want them to like her.

Taking out her compact, she carefully polished her eyeballs. The man at the controls of the machine practically performed a ritual *entrechat*.

"Don't do that!" Stet ordered in a harsh whisper.

"But why not?" she asked, unable to restrain a trace of belligerence from her voice. He hadn't been very polite himself. "The handbook said respectable Terran women make up in public. Why shouldn't I?"

He sighed. "It'll take time for you to catch on, I suppose. There's a lot the handbook doesn't—can't—cover. You'll find the setup here rather different from on Fizbus," he went on as he kicked open the door neatly lettered *THE FIZBUS TIMES* in both Fizbian and Terran. "We've found it expedient to follow the local newspaper practice. For instance—" he indicated a small green-feathered man seated at a desk just beyond the railing that bisected the room horizontally—"we have a Copy Editor."

"What does he do?" she asked, confused.

"He copies news from the other papers, of course."

"And what are *you* doing tonight, Miss Morfatch?" the Copy Editor asked, springing up from his desk to execute the three ritual entrechats with somewhat more verve than was absolutely necessary.

"Having dinner with me," Stet said quickly.

"Pulling rank, eh, old bird? Well, we'll see whether position or sterling worth will win out in the end."

As the rest of the staff crowded around Tarb, leaping and booing as appreciatively as any girl could want, she managed to snatch a rapid look around. The place wasn't really so very much different from a Fizbian newsroom, once she got over the oddity of going across, not up and down, with the desks—queerly shaped but undeniably desks—arranged side by side instead of one over the other. There were chairs and stools, no perches, but that was to be expected in a wingless society. And it was noisy. Even though the little machines had stopped clattering when she came in, a distant roaring continued, as if, concealed somewhere close by, larger, more sinister machines continued their work. A peculiar smell hung in the air—not unpleasant, exactly, but strange.

She sniffed inquiringly.

"Ink," Stet said.

"What's that?"

"Oh, some stuff the boys in the back shop use. The feature writers," he went on quickly, before she could ask what the "back shop" was, "have private offices where they can perch in comfort."

He led the way down a corridor, opening doors. "Our drama editor." He indicated a middle-aged man with faded blue feathers, who hung head downward from his perch. "On the lobster-trick last night writing a review, so he's catching fifty-one twinkles now."

"Enchanted, Miss Morfatch," the critic said, opening one bright eye. "By a curious chance, it so happens that tonight I have two tickets to—"

"Tonight she's going out with me."

"Well, I can get tickets to any play, any night. And you haven't laughed unless you've seen a Terrestrial drama. Just say the word, chick."

Stet got Tarb out of the office and slammed the door shut. "Over here is the office of our food editor," he said, breathing hard, "whom you'll be expected to give a claw to now and then, since your jobs overlap. Can't introduce you to him right now, though, because he's in the hospital with ptomaine poisoning. And this is the office you'll share with Drosmig."

Stet opened the door.

Underneath the perch, Senbot Drosmig, dean of Fizbian journalists, lay on the rug in a sodden stupor, letters to the editor scattered thickly over his shriveled person. The whole room reeked unmistakably of caffeine.

Tarb shrank back and twined both feet around Stet's. This time he did not repulse her. "But how can a—an educated, cultured man like Senbot Drosmig sink to such depths?"

"It's hard for anyone with even the slightest inclination toward the stuff to resist it here," Stet replied somberly. "I can't deny it; the sale of caffeine is absolutely unrestricted on Earth. Coffee shops all over the place. Coffee served freely at even the best homes. And not only coffee . . . caffeine is insiduously present in other of their popular beverages."

Her eyes bulged sideways. "But how can a so-called civilized people be so depraved?"

"Caffeine doesn't seem to affect them the way it does us. Their nervous systems are so very uncomplicated, one almost envies them."

Drosmig stirred restlessly under his blanket of correspondence. "Go back . . . Fizbus," he muttered. "Warn you . . . 'fore . . . too late . . . like me."

Tarb's rose-pink feathers stood on end. She looked apprehensively at Stet.

"Senbot can't go back because he's in no shape to take the interstel drive." The young editor was obviously annoyed. "He's old and he's a physical wreck. But that certainly doesn't apply to you, Miss Morfatch." He looked long and hard into her eyes.

"Few years on planet," Drosmig groaned, struggling to his wings, "'ply to anybody."

His feathers, Tarb noticed, were an ugly, darkish brown. She had never seen any one that color before, but she'd heard rumors that too much caffeine could do that to you. At least she hoped it was only the caffeine.

"For your information, he was almost as bad as this when he came!" Stet snapped. "Frankly, that's why he was sent here—to get rid of his unfortunate addiction. Grupe had no idea, when he assigned him to Earth, that there was caffeine on the planet."

The old man gave a sardonic laugh as he clumsily made his way to the perch and gripped it with quivering toes.

"That is, I don't *think* he knew," Stet said dubiously.

Tarb reached over and picked a letter off the floor. The Fizbian characters were clumsy and ill-made, as if someone had formed them with his feet. Could there be such poverty here that individuals existed who could not afford a scripto? The letter didn't read like any that had ever been printed in the column—at least none that had been picked up in the Fizbus edition:

*

New York

Dear Senbot Drosmig:

I am a subaltern clerk in the shipping department of the FizbEarth Trading Company, Inc. Although I have held this post for only three months, I have already won the respect and esteem of my superiors through my diligence and good character. My habits are exemplary: I do not gamble, sing, or take caffeine.

Earlier today, while engaged in evening meditation at my modest apartments, I was aroused by a peremptory knock at the door. I flung it open. A native stood there with a small case in his hand.

"Is the house on fire?" I asked, wondering which of my few humble possessions I should rescue first.

"No," he said. "I would like to interest you in some brushes."

"Are the offices of the FizbEarth Trading Company, Inc., on fire?"

"Not to my knowledge," he replied, opening his case. "Now I have here a very nice hairbrush—"

I wanted to give him every chance. "Have you come to tell me of any disaster relative to the FizbEarth Trading Company, to myself, or to anyone or anything else with whom or with which I am connected?"

"Why, no," he said. "I have come to sell you brushes. Now here is a little number I know you'll like. My company developed it with you folks specially in mind. It's—"

"Do you know, sir, that you have wantonly interrupted me in the midst of my meditations, which constitutes an established act of privacy violation?"

"Is that a fact? Now this little item is particularly designed for brushing the wings—"

At that point, I knocked him down and punched him into insensibility with my feet. Then I summoned the police. To my surprise, they arrested me instead of him.

I am writing this letter from jail. I do not like to ask my employers to get me out because, even though I am innocent, you know how a thing like this can leave a smudge on the record.

What shall I do?

Anxiously yours,

Fruzmus Bloxx

*

"What should he do?" Tarb asked, handing Stet the paper. "Or is the question academic by now? The letter's five days old."

Stet sighed. "I'll find out whether the consulate has been notified. Native police usually do that, you know. Very thoughtful fellows. If this Bloxx hasn't been bailed out already, I'll see that he is."

"But how will we answer his letter? Advise him to sue for false arrest?"

Stet smiled. "But he has no grounds for false arrest. He is guilty of assault. The native was entirely within his rights in trying to sell him a brush. Now—" he put out a foot—"brace yourself. Privacy violation is not a crime on Terra. It is perfectly legal. In fact, it does not exist as such!"

At that point, everything went maroon.

When Tarb came to, she found herself lying upon Drosmig's desk. A skin-faced native woman was offering her water and clucking.

"Are you all right, Tarb—Miss Morfatch?" Stet demanded anxiously.

"Yes. I—I think so," she murmured, raising herself to a crouch.

"Better . . . have died," Drosmig groaned from his perch. "Fate worse . . . death . . . awaits you."

Tarb tried to smile. "Sorry to have been so much trouble." She stuck out her tongue at both Stet and the native.

The woman drew in her breath.

"Miss Morfatch," Stet reminded Tarb, "sticking out the tongue is not an apology on Terra; it is an insult. Fortunately, Miss Snow happens to be perhaps the only Terran who would not be offended. She has become thoroughly acquainted with us and our odd little customs. She even—" he beamed at the Terran female—"has learned to speak our language."

"Hail to thee, O visitor from the stars," Miss Snow said in Fizbian. "May thy sojourn upon Earth be an incessant delight and may peace and plenty shower their gifts in abundance upon thee."

Tarb put her hand to her aching head. "I'm very glad to meet you," she said, glad she did not have to get up to make the ritual *entrechats*.

"Miss Snow is my right foot," Stet said, "but I'm going to be noble and let her act as your secretary until you can learn to operate a typewriter."

"Secretary? Typewriter?"

"Well, you see, there are no scriptos or superscriptos on Earth and we can't import any from Home because the natives—" Miss Snow smiled—"don't have the right kind of power here to run psychic installations. All prosifying has to be done directly on prosifying machines or—" he paused—"by foot."

"Catch her!" Miss Snow exclaimed in Terran.

Everything had gone maroon for Tarb again. As she fell, she could hear a sudden thump. It was, she later discovered, Drosmig falling off his perch again—the result of insecure grip, she was given to understand, rather than excessive empathy.

*

"I didn't mean, of course, to give you the impression that we actually produce the individual copies of the papers ourselves," Stet explained over the dinner table that night. "We have native printers who do that. They've turned out some really remarkable Fizbian type fonts." "Very clever of them," Tarb said, knowing that was what she was expected to say. She glanced around the restaurant. In their low-cut evening garments, the Terrestrial females looked much less Fizboid than they had during the day. All that naked-looking skin; one would think they'd want to cover it. Probably they were sick with jealousy of her beautiful rose-colored down—what they could see of it, anyway.

"Of course, our real problem is getting proofreaders. The proofing machines won't operate here either, of course, and so we need human personnel. But what Fizbian would do such degrading work? We had thought of convict labor, but—"

"Why mustn't I take off my wrap?" Tarb interrupted. "No one else is wearing one."

Stet coughed. "You'll feel much less self-conscious about your wings if you keep it on. And try not to use your feet so conspicuously. I'm sure everyone understands you need them to eat with, but—"

"But I'm not in the least self-conscious about my wings. On Fizbus, they were considered rather nice-looking, if I do say so myself."

"It's better," he said firmly, "not to emphasize the differences between the natives and ourselves. You didn't object to wearing a Terrestrial costume, did you?"

"No, I realize I must make some concessions to native prudery, but—"

"Matter of fact, I've been thinking it would be a good idea for you to wear a stole or a cape or something in the daytime when you go to and from the office. You wouldn't want to make yourself or the *Times* conspicuous, I'm sure. . . . No, waiter, no coffee. We'll take champagne."

"I want to try coffee," Tarb said mutinously. "Champagne! You'd think I was a fledgling, giving me that bubbly stuff!"

He looked at her. "Now don't be silly, Miss Morfatch . . . Tarb. I can't let you indulge in such rash experiments. You realize I am responsible for you."

Tarb muttered darkly into her *coupe maison*.

Stet raised his eyebrows. "What did you say?"

"I was only wondering whether you'd remembered to check on whether that young man—Bloxx—ever did get out of jail."

Stet snapped his toes. "Glad you reminded me. Completely slipped my mind. Let's go and see what happened to him, shall we?"

*

As they rose to leave, a dumpy Earthwoman rushed up to them, enthusiastically babbling in Terran. Seizing Tarb's foot, she clung to it before the Fizbian girl could do anything to prevent her. Tarb had to spread her wings wide to retain her balance. Her cloak flew off and an adjoining table of diners disappeared beneath it.

Stet and the headwaiter rushed to the rescue with profuse apologies, Stet's crest undulating as if it concealed a nest of snakes. But Tarb was too much frightened to be calmed.

"Is this a hostile attack?" she shrieked frantically at Stet. "Because the handbook never said shaking feet was an Earth custom!"

"No, no, she's a friend!" Stet yelled, leaving the diners still struggling with the cloak as he sped back to her. "And shaking feet isn't an Earth custom; she thinks it's a Fizbian one. You see. . . . Oh, hell, never mind—I'll explain the whole thing to you later. But she's just greeting you, trying to put you at your ease. It's Belinda Romney, a very important Terrestrial. She owns the Solar Press—you must have heard of it even on Fizbus—biggest news service on the planet. Absolutely wouldn't do to offend her. Mrs. Romney, may I present Miss Morfatch?"

The woman beamed and continued to gush endlessly.

"Tell her to let go my foot!" Tarb demanded. "It's getting so it feels carbonated."

He smiled deprecatingly. "Now, Tarb, we mustn't be rude—"

For the first time in her life, Tarb spoke Terran to a Terrestrial. She formed the words slowly and carefully: "Sorry we must leave, but we have to go to jail."

She looked to Stet for approval . . . and didn't get it. He started to explain something quickly to the woman. Every time she'd heard him speak Terran, Tarb thought, he seemed to be introducing, explaining or apologizing.

It turned out that, through some oversight, the usually thoughtful Terran police department had neglected to inform the Fizbian consul that one of his people had been incarcerated, for the young man had already been tried, found guilty of assault plus contempt of court, and sentenced to pay a large fine. However, after Stet had given his version of the circumstances to a sympathetic judge, the sum was reduced to a nominal one, which the *Times* paid.

"But I don't see why you should have paid anything at all," Bloxx protested ungratefully. "I didn't do anything wrong. You should have made an issue of it."

"According to Earth laws, you did do wrong," Stet said wearily, "and this is Earth. What's more, if we take the matter up, it will naturally get into print. You don't want your employers to hear about it, do you—even if you don't care about making Fizbians look ridiculous to Terrestrials?"

"I suppose I wouldn't like FizbEarth to find out," Bloxx conceded. "As it is, I'll have to do some fast explaining to account for my not having shown up for nearly a week. I'll say I caught some horrible Earth disease—that'll scare them so much, they'll probably beg me to take another week off. Though I do wish you fellows over at the *Times* would answer your mail sooner. I'm a regular subscriber, you know."

*

"But the same kind of thing's going to happen over and over again, isn't it, Stet?" Tarb asked as a taxi took them back to the hotel in which most of the *Times* staff was domiciled. "If privacy doesn't exist on Earth, it's bound to keep occurring."

"Eh?" Stet took his attention away from her toes with some difficulty. "Some Earth people like privacy, too, but they have to fight for it. Violations aren't legally punishable—that's the only difference."

"Then surely the Terrestrials would understand about us, wouldn't they?" she asked eagerly. "If they knew how strongly we felt about privacy, maybe they wouldn't violate it—not as much, anyway. I'm sure they're not vicious, just ignorant. And you can't just keep on getting Fizbians out of jail each time they run up against the problem. It would be too expensive, for one thing."

"Don't worry," he said, pressing her toes. "I'll take care of the whole thing."

"An article in the paper wouldn't really help much," she persisted thoughtfully, "and I suppose you must have run at least one already. It would explain to the Fizbians that Terrestrials don't regard invasion of privacy as a crime, but it wouldn't tell the Terrestrials that Fizbians do. We'll have to think of—"

"You're surely not going to tell me how to run my paper on your first day here, are you?"

He tried to take the sting out of his words by twining his toes around hers, but she felt guilty. She had been presumptuous. Probably there were lots of things she couldn't understand yet—like why she shouldn't polish her eyeballs in public. Stet had finally explained to her that, while Terrestrial women did make up in public, they didn't scour their irises, ever, and would be startled and horrified to see someone else doing so.

"But I was horrified to see them raking their feathers in public!" Tarb had contended.

"Combing their hair, my dear. And why not? This is their planet."

That was always his answer. *I wonder*, she speculated, *whether he would expect a Terrestrial visitor to Fizbus to fly . . . because, after all, Fizbus is our planet.* But she didn't dare broach the question.

However, if it was presumptuous of her to make helpful suggestions the first day, it was more than presumptuous of Stet to ask her up to his rooms to see his collection of rare early twentieth-century Terrestrial milk bottles and other antiques. So she just told him courteously that she was tired and wanted to go to roost. And, since the hotel had a whole section fitted up to suit Fizbian requirements, she spent a more comfortable night than she had expected.

She awoke the next day full of enthusiasm and ready to start in on the great work at once. Although she might have been a little too forward the previous night, she knew, as she took a reassuring glance in the mirror, that Stet would forgive her.

*

In the office, she was, at first, somewhat self-conscious about Drosmig, who hung insecurely from his perch muttering to himself, but she soon forgot him in her preoccupation with duty. The first letter she picked up—although again oddly unlike the ones she'd read in the paper on Fizbus—seemed so simple that she felt she would have no difficulty in answering it all by herself:

Heidelberg

Dear Senbot Drosmig:

I am a professor of Fizbian History at a local university. Since my salary is a small one, owing to the small esteem in which the natives hold culture, I must economize wherever I can in order to make both ends meet. Accordingly, I do my own cooking and shop at the self-service supermarket around the corner, where I have found that prices are lower than in the service groceries and the food no worse.

However, the manager and a number of the customers have objected to my shopping with my feet. They don't so much mind my taking packages off the shelves with them, but they have been quite vociferous on the subject of my pinching the fruit with my toes. Unripe fruit, however, makes me ill. What shall I do?

Sincerely yours,

Grez B'Groot

Tarb dictated an unhesitating reply:

Dear Professor B'Groot:

Why don't you explain to the manager of the store that Fizbians have wings and feet rather than arms and hands?

I'm sure his attitude and the attitudes of his customers will change when they learn that your pinching the fruit with your feet is not mere pedagogical eccentricity, but the regular practice on our planet. Point out to him that your feet are covered and, therefore, more sanitary than the bare hands of his other customers.

And always put on clean socks before you go shopping.

Helpfully yours,

Senbot Drosmig

Miss Snow raised pale eyebrows.

"Is something wrong?" Tarb asked anxiously. "Should I have put in that bit about work, study, meditate? It seems inappropriate somehow."

"Oh, no, not that. It's just that your letter—well, violates Mr. Zarnon's precept that, in Rome, one must do as the Romans do."

"But this isn't Rome," Tarb replied, bewildered. "It's New York."

"He didn't make the saying up," Miss Snow replied testily. "It's a Terrestrial proverb."

"Oh," Tarb said.

She resented this creature's trying to tell her how to do her job. On the other hand, Tarb was wise enough to realize that Miss Snow, unpleasant though she might be, probably did know Stet well enough to be able to predict his reactions.

So Tarb not only was reluctant to show Stet what she had already done, but hesitated about answering another and even more urgent letter that had just been brought in by special messenger. She tried to compromise by submitting the letters to Drosmig—for, technically speaking, it was he who was her immediate superior—but he merely groaned, "Tell 'em all to drop dead," from his perch and refused to open his eyes.

In the end, Tarb had to take the letters to Stet's office. Miss Snow trailed along behind her, uninvited. And, since this was a place of business, Tarb could not claim a privacy violation. Even if it weren't a place of business, she remembered, she couldn't—not here on Earth. Advanced spirituality, hah!

Advanced pain in the pinions!

Stet read the first letter and her answer smilingly. "Excellent, Tarb—" her hearts leaped—"for a first try, but I'd like to suggest a few changes, if I may."

"Well, of course," she said, pretending not to notice the smirk on Miss Snow's face.

"Just write this Professor B'Goot that he should do his shopping at a grocery that offers service and practice his economies elsewhere. A professor, of all people, is expected to uphold the dignity of his own race—the idea, sneering at a culture that was thousands of years old when we were still building nests! Terrestrials couldn't possibly have any respect for him if they saw him prodding kumquats with his toes."

"It's no sillier than writing with one's vestigial wings!" Tarb blazed.

"Well!" Miss Snow exclaimed in Terran. "Well, *really*!"

Tarb started to stick out her tongue, then remembered. "I didn't mean to offend you, Miss Snow. I know it's your custom. But wouldn't you understand if I typewrote with my feet?"

Miss Snow tittered.

"If you want the honest truth, hon, it would make you look like a feathered monkey."

"If you want the honest truth about what you look like to me, dearie—it's a plucked chicken!"

"Tarb, I think you should apologize to Miss Snow!"

"All right!" Tarb stuck out her tongue. Miss Snow promptly thrust out hers in return.

"Ladies, ladies!" Stet cried. "I think there has been a slight confusion of folkways!" He quickly changed the subject. "Is that another letter you have there, Tarb?"

"Yes, but I didn't try to answer it. I thought you'd better have a look at it first, since Miss Snow didn't seem to think much of the job I did with the other one."

"Miss Snow always has the *Times*' welfare at heart," Stet remarked ambiguously, and read:

Chicago

Dear Senbot Drosmig:

I am employed as translator by the extraterrestrial division of Burns and Deerhart, Inc., the well-known interstellar mail-order house. As the company employs no other Fizbians and our offices are situated in a small rural community where no others of our race reside, I find myself rather lonely. Moreover, being a bachelor, with neither chick nor child on Fizbus, I have nothing to look forward to upon my return to the Home Planet some day.

Accordingly, I decided to adopt a child to cheer my declining years. I dispatched an interstellargram to a reliable orphanage on Fizbus, outlining my hopes and requirements in some detail. After they had satisfied themselves as to my income, strength of character, etc., they sent me a fatherless and motherless egg in cold storage, which I was supposed to hatch upon arrival.

However, when the egg came to Earth, it was impounded by Customs. They say it is forbidden to import extrasolar eggs. I have tried to explain to them that it is not at all a question of importation but of adoption; however, they cannot or will not understand.

Please tell me what to do. I fear that they may not be keeping the egg at the correct Fizbian freezing point—which, as you know, is a good deal lower than Earth's. The fledgling may hatch by itself and receive a traumatic shock that might very well damage its entire psyche permanently.

Frantically yours,

Glibmus Gluyt

"Oh, for the stars' sake!" Stet exploded. "This is really too much! Viz our consul, Miss Snow. That egg must go back to Fizbus at once, before any Terrestrials hear of it! And I must notify the government back on the Home Planet to keep a close check on all egg shipments. Something like this must certainly not occur again."

"Why shouldn't the Terrestrials hear of it?" Tarb asked, outraged. "And I think it's mean of you to send back a poor little orphan egg like that when it has a chance of getting a good home."

"An egg!" Miss Snow repeated incredulously. "You mean you really. . . ?" She gave me one mad little hoot of laughter and then stopped and strangled slightly. Her face turned purple in her efforts to restrain mirth. *Really*, Tarb thought, *she looks so much better that color.*

Stet's crest twitched violently. "I hope—" he began. "I do hope you will keep this . . . knowledge to yourself, Miss Snow."

"But of course," she assured him, calming down. "I'm dreadfully sorry I was so rude. Naturally I wouldn't dream of telling a soul, Mr. Zarnon. You can trust me."

"I'm sure I can, Miss Snow."

Tarb almost choked with indignation. "You mean you've been keeping the facts of our life from Terrestrials? As if they were fledglings . . . no, even fledglings are told these days."

"One could hardly blame him for it, Miss Morfatch," Miss Snow said. "You wouldn't want people to know that Fizbians laid eggs, would you?"

"And why not?"

"Tarb," Stet intervened, "you don't know what you're talking about."

"Oh, don't I? You're ashamed of the fact that we bear our children in a clean, decent, honorable way instead of—" She stopped. "I'm being as bad as you two are. Probably the Terrestrials' way of reproduction doesn't seem dirty to them—but, since they do reproduce *that* way, they could scarcely find our way objectionable!"

"Tarb, that's not how a young girl should talk!"

"Oh, go lay an egg!" she said, knowing that she had overstepped the limits of propriety, but unable to let him get away with that. "I hope to be a wife and mother some day," she added, "and I only hope that when that time comes, I'll be able to lay good eggs."

"Miss Morfatch," Stet said, keeping control of his temper with a visible effort, "that will be enough from you. If common decency doesn't restrain you, please remember that I am your employer and that *I* set the policies on *my* paper. You'll do what you're told and keep a civil tongue in your head or you'll be sent back to Fizbus. Do I make myself clear?"

"You do, indeed," Tarb said. How could she ever have thought he was charming and handsome? Well, perhaps he still was handsome, but fine feathers do not make fine deeds. And, if it came to that, it wasn't his paper.

"We have the same thing on Terra," Miss Snow murmured sympathetically to Stet. "These young whippersnappers think they can start in running the paper the very first day. Why, Belinda Romney herself—she's a distant cousin of mine, you know—told me—"

"Miss Snow," Tarb said, "I hope for the sake of Earth that you are not a typical example of the Terrestrial species."

"And you, hon," Miss Snow retorted, "don't belong on a paper, but in a chicken coop."

"Ladies!" Stet said helplessly. "Women," he muttered, "certainly do not belong on a newspaper. Matter of fact, they don't belong anywhere; their place is in the home only because there's nowhere else to put them."

Both females glared at him.

*

During the next fortnight, Tarb gained fluency in Terran and also learned to operate a Terrestrial typewriter equipped with Fizbian type—mostly so that she could dispense with the services of the invaluable Miss Snow. She didn't like typing, though—it chipped her toenails and her temper. Besides, Drosmig kept complaining that the noise prevented him from sleeping and she preferred him to sleep rather than hang there making irrelevant and, sometimes, unpleasantly relevant remarks.

"Longing for the old scripto, eh?" one of the cameramen smiled as he lounged in the open doorway of her office. Although she was fond of fresh air, Tarb realized that she would have to keep the door shut from now on. Too many of the younger members of the staff kept booing at her as they passed, and now they had formed the habit of dropping in to offer her advice, encouragement and invitations to meals. At first, the attention had pleased her—but now she was much too busy to be bothered; she was going to turn out acceptable answers to those letters or die trying.

"Well, if the power can't be converted, it can't," she said grimly. "Griblo, I do wish you'd be a dear and flutter off. I—"

He snorted. "Who says the power can't be converted? Stet, huh?"

She took her feet off the keys and looked at him. "Why do you say 'Stet' that way?"

"Because that's a lot of birdseed he gives you about not being able to convert Earth power. Could be done all right, but he and the consul have it all fixed up to keep Fizbian technology off the planet. Consul's probably being paid off by the International Association of Manufacturers and Stet's in it for the preservation of indigenous culture—and maybe a little cash, too. After all, those rare antique collections of his cost money."

"I don't believe it!" Tarb snapped. "Griblo, please—I have so much work to get through!"

"Okay, chick, but I warn you, you're going to have your bright-eyed illusions shattered. Why don't you wake up to the truth about Stet? What you should do is maybe eschew the society of all journalists entirely, and a sordid lot they are, and devote yourself to photographers—splendid fellows, all."

"Please shut the door behind you!"

The door slammed.

Tarb gazed disconsolately at the letter before her. Would she ever be able to answer letters to Stet's satisfaction? The purpose of the whole column was service—but did she and Stet mean the same thing by the same word? Or, if they did, whom was Stet serving?

She was paying too much attention to Griblo's idle remarks. Obviously he was a sorehead—had some kind of grudge against Stet. Perhaps Stet was a bit too autocratic, perhaps he had even gone native to some extent, but you couldn't say anything worse about him than that. All in all, he wasn't a bad bird and she mustn't let herself be influenced by rumormongers like Griblo.

*

Tarb got up and took the letter to Stet. He was in his office dictating to Miss Snow. *After all*, Tarb could not repress the ugly thought, *why should he care about the scriptos? He'll never have to use a typewriter.*

And he was perfectly nice about being interrupted. The only thing he didn't like was being contradicted. *I'm getting bitter*, she told herself in surprise. *And at my age, too. I wonder what I'll be like when I'm old.*

This thought alarmed her and so she smiled very sweetly at Stet as she murmured, "Would you mind reading this?" and gave him the letter.

"Run into another little snag, eh?" he said affably, giving her foot a gentle pat with his. "Well, let's see what we can do about it."

Montreal

Dear Senbot Drosmig:

I am a chef at the Cafe Inter-stellaire, which, as everyone knows, is one of the most chic eating establishments on this not very chic planet. During my spare moments, I am a great amateur of the local form of entertainment known as television. I am especially fascinated by the native actress Ingeborg Swedenborg, who, in spite of being a Terran, compares most favorably with our own Fizbian footlight favorites.

The other day, while I am in the kitchen engaged in preparing the ragout celeste à la fizbe for which I am justly celebrated on nine planets, I hear a stir outside in the dining room. I strain my ears. I hear the cry, "It is Ingeborg Swedenborg!"

I cannot help myself. I rush to the doorway. There, behold, the incomparable Ingeborg herself! She follows the headwaiter to a choice table. She is even more ravishing in real life than on the screen. On her, it does not matter that she has no feathers save on the head—even skin looks good. Overcome by involuntary ardor, I boo at her. Whereupon I am violently assailed by a powerfully built native whom I have not previously noticed to be escorting her.

I am rescued before he can do me any permanent damage, though, if you wish the truth, it will be a long time before I can fly again. However, I am given notice by the cold-hearted management. Now I am without a job. And what is more, if on this planet one is not permitted to express one's instinctive and natural admiration for a beautiful woman, then all I have to say is that it is a lousy planet and I wiggle my toes at it. How do I go about getting deported?

Impatiently yours,

Rajois Sludd

"Oh, I suppose it serves him right," Tarb said quickly, before Stet could comment, "but don't you think it would be a good idea if the *Times* got up a Fizbian-Terrestrial handbook of its own? It's the only solution that I can see. The regular one, I recognize now, is more than inadequate, with all that spiritual gup—" Miss Snow drew in her breath sharply—"and not much else. All these problems are bound to arise again and again. Frankly speaking, Stet, your solutions only take care of the individual cases; they don't establish a sound intercultural basis."

He grunted.

"What's more," she went on eagerly, "we could not only give copies to every Fizbian planning to visit Earth, but also print copies in Terran for Terrestrials who are interested in learning more about Fizbus and the Fizbians. In fact, all Terrans who come in contact with us should have the book. It would help both races to understand each other so much better and—"

"Unnecessary!" Stet snapped, so violently that she stopped with her mouth open. "The standard handbook is more than adequate. Whatever limitations it may have are deliberate. Setting down in cold print all that . . . stuff you want to have included would make a point of things we prefer not to stress. I wouldn't want to have the Terrestrials humor me as if I were a fledgling or a foreigner."

He leaped out of his chair and paced up and down the office. One would think he had forgotten he ever could fly.

"But you are a foreigner, Stet," Tarb said gently. "No matter what you do or say, Terrestrials and Fizbians are—well, worlds apart."

"Spiritually, I am much closer to the Terrestrials than—but you wouldn't understand." He and Miss Snow nodded sympathetically at each other. "And you might be interested to know that I happen to be the author of all that 'spiritual gup.' I wrote the handbook—as a service to Fizbus, I might point out. I wasn't paid for it."

"Oh, dear!" Tarb said. "Oh, *dear*! I really and truly am sorry, Stet."

He brushed her apologies aside. "Answer that letter. Ignore the question about deportation entirely." He ran a foot through his crest. "Just tell the fellow to see our personnel manager. We could use a chef in the company dining room. Haven't tasted a decent celestial ragout—at a price I could afford—since I left Fizbus."

"Would you want me to print that reply in the column?" she asked. "'If you lose your job because you're unfamiliar with Terrestrial customs, come to the *Times*. We'll give you another job at a much lower salary.'"

"Of course not! Send your answer directly to him. You don't think we put any of those letters you've been answering in the column, do you? Or any that come in at all, for that matter. I have to write all the letters that are printed—and answer them myself."

"I should have recognized the style," Tarb said. "So this is the service the *Times* offers to its subscribers. Nothing that would be of help. Nothing that could prevent other Fizbians from making the same mistake. Nothing that could be controversial. Nothing that would help Terrestrials to understand us. Nothing, in short, but a lot of birdseed!"

"Impertinence!" Miss Snow remarked. "You shouldn't let her talk to you like that, Mr. Zarnon."

"Tarb!" Stet roared, casting an impatient glance at Miss Snow. "How dare you talk to me in that way? And all this is none of your business, anyway."

"I'm a Fizbian," she stated, "and it certainly is my business. I'm not ashamed of having wings. I'm proud of them and sorry for people who don't have them. And, by the stars, I'm going to fly. If skirts are improper to wear for flying, then I can wear slacks. I saw them in a Terrestrial fashion magazine and they're perfectly respectable."

"Not for working hours," Miss Snow sniffed.

"I have no intention of flying during working hours," Tarb snapped back. "Even you should be able to see that the ceiling's much too low."

Stet ran a foot through his crest again. "I hate to say this, Tarb, but I don't feel you're the right person for this job. You mean well, I'm sure, but you're too—too inflexible."

"You mean I have principles," she retorted, "and you don't." Which wasn't entirely true; he had principles—it was just that they were unprincipled.

"That will be enough, Tarb," he said sternly. "You'd better go now while I think this over. I'd hate to send you back to Fizbus, because I'd—well, I'd miss you. On the other hand. . . . "

Tarb went back to her office and drafted a long interstel to a cousin on Fizbus, explaining what she would like for a birthday present. "And send it special delivery," she concluded, "because I am having an urgent and early birthday."

*

"Tarb Morfatch!" Stet howled, a few months later. "What on Earth are you doing?"

"Dictating into my scripto," Tarb said cheerfully. "Some of the boys from the print shop helped fix it up for me. They were very nice about it, too, considering that the superscriptos will probably throw them out of work. You know, Stet, Terrestrials can be quite decent people."

"Where did you get that scripto?"

"Cousin Mylfis sent it to me for my birthday. I must have complained about wearing out my claws on a typewriter and he didn't understand that scriptos won't work on Earth. Only they do." She beamed at her employer. "All it needed was a transformer. I guess you're just not mechanically minded, Stet."

He clenched his feet. "Tarb, Terrestrials aren't ready for our technology. You've done a very unwise thing in having that scripto sent to you. And I've done a very unwise thing in keeping you here against my better judgment."

"Maybe the Terrestrials aren't ready," she said, ignoring his last remark, "but I'm not going to wear my feet to the bone if I can get a gadget that'll do the same thing with no expenditure of physical energy." She placed a foot on his. "I don't see how a thing like this could possibly corrupt the Terrestrials, Stet. It's made a better, brighter girl out of me already."

"Hear, hear!" said Drosmig hoarsely from his perch.

"Shut up, Senbot. You just don't understand, Tarb. If you'll only—"

"But I'm afraid I do understand, Stet. And I won't send my scripto back."

"May I come in?" Miss Snow tapped lightly on the door frame. "Is what I hear true?"

"About the scripto?" Tarb asked. "It certainly is. All you have to do is talk into it and the words appear on the paper. Guess that makes you obsolete, doesn't it, Miss Snow?"

"And high time, too," commented Drosmig. "Never liked the old biddy."

"Senbot. . . . " Stet began, and stopped. "Oh, what's the use trying to talk reasonably to either of you! Tarb, come back to my office with me."

She could not refuse and so she followed. Miss Snow, torn between curiosity and the scripto, hesitated and then made after them.

"I've decided to take you off the column—for this morning, anyway—and send you on an outside assignment," Stet told Tarb. "The consul's wife is coming to Earth today. Once she heard there was another woman on Terra, nothing could stop her. Consul seems to think it's my fault, too," he added moodily. "Won't believe I had nothing to do with hiring you. I told the Home Office not to send a woman, that she'd disrupt the office, and you sure as hell have."

"But I thought you said in your letters that you were doing everything in your power to bring Fizbian womenfolk to their men on Terra!" Tarb pointed out malevolently.

"Yes," he confessed. "We must please our readers. You know that. Anyway, all that's irrelevant right now. What I want you to do is go meet the consul's wife. Nice touch, having the only other Fizbian woman here be the one to interview her. Human interest angle for the Terrestrial papers. Shouldn't be surprised if Solar Press picked it up—they like items of that kind for fillers. Take Griblo along with you and make sure he has film in his camera this time."

"Yes, sir," Tarb said. "Anything you say, sir."

He pretended not to notice her sarcasm. "I have a list of the questions you should ask her." He fixed her with his eye. "You stick to them, do you hear me? I don't want anything controversial." He rummaged among the papers on his desk. "I know I had it half an hour ago. Sit down, will you, Tarb? Stop hopping around."

"If I can't have a perch, I want a stool," Tarb said. "This is a private office and I think it's a gross affectation for you to have those silly, uncomfortable chairs in it."

"If you would have your wings clipped like Mr. Zarnon's—" Miss Snow began before Stet could stop her.

"Stet, you *didn't*!"

His crest thrashed back and forth. "They'll grow back again and it's so much more convenient this way. After all, I can't use them here and I do have to associate with Terrestrials and use their equipment. The consul has had his wings clipped also and so have several of our more prominent industrialists—"

"Oh, *Stet*!" Tarb wailed. "I was beginning to think some pretty hard things about you, but I wouldn't ever have dreamed you'd do anything as awful as that!"

"Why should I have to apologize to you?" he raged. "Who do you think you are, anyway? You're an incompetent little fool. I should have fired you that first day. I've let you get away with so much only because you have a pretty face. You've only been on Earth a couple of months; how can you presume to think you know what's good and what's bad for the Fizbians here?"

"I may not know what's good," she retorted, "but I certainly do know what's bad. And that's you, Stet—you and everything you stand for. You not only don't have the courage of your convictions, you don't even have any convictions. You're ashamed of being a Fizbian, ashamed of anything that makes Fizbians different from Terrestrials, even if it's something better, something that most Terrans would like to have. You're a damned hypocrite, Stet Zarnon, that's what you are—professing to help our people when actually you're hurting them by trying to force them into the mold of an alien species."

She brushed back her crest. "I take it I'm fired," she said more quietly. "Do you want me to interview the consul's wife first or leave right away?"

It took Stet a moment to bring his voice under control. "Interview her first. We'll talk this over when you get back."

*

It was pleasant to be away from the office, she thought as the taxi pulled toward the airfield, and doing wingwork again, even if it proved to be the first and last time on this planet. Griblo sat hunched in a corner of the seat, too preoccupied with the camera, which, even after two years, he hadn't fully mastered, to pay attention to her.

Outside, it was raining, the kind of thin drizzle that, on Fizbus or Earth, could go on for days. Tarb had brought along the native umbrella she had purchased in the hotel gift shop—a delightful contraption that was supposed to keep off the rain and didn't, and was supposed to collapse and did, but at the wrong moments. She planned to take it back with her when she returned to Fizbus. Approved souvenir or not, it was the same beautiful purple as her eyes. And, besides, who had made the ruling about approved souvenirs? Stet, of course.

"No reason why we couldn't have autofax brought from Home," Griblo suddenly grumbled.

Tarb pulled herself back from her thoughts. "I suppose Stet wouldn't let you," she said. "But now that one scripto's here," she went on somewhat complacently, "he'll have to—"

"Keep this planet charming and unspoiled, he says," Griblo interrupted ungratefully. "Its spiritual values will be corrupted by too much contact with a crass advanced technology. And, of course, he's got the local camera manufacturers solidly behind him. I wonder whether they advertise in the *Times* because he helps keep autofax off Terra or whether he keeps the autofax off Terra because they advertise in the *Times*."

"But what does he care about advertising? He may talk as if he owned the *Times*, but he doesn't."

Griblo gave a nasty laugh. "No, he doesn't, but if the Terran edition didn't show a profit, it'd fold quicker than you can flip your wings and he'd have to go back to nasty old up-to-date Fizbus as a lowly sub-editor. And he wouldn't like that one bit. Our Stet, as you may have noticed, is fond of running things to suit himself."

"But Mr. Grupe told me that the *Times* isn't interested in money. It's running this edition of the paper only as a service to—oh, I suppose all that was a lot of birdseed, too!"

"Grupe!" Griblo snorted. "The sanctimonious old buzzard! He's a big stockholder on the paper. Bet you didn't know that, did you? All they're out for is money. Fizbian money, Terrestrial money—so long as it's cash."

"Tell me, Griblo," Tarb asked, "what does 'When in Rome, do as the Romans do' mean?"

Griblo grinned sourly. "Stet's favorite motto." He moved along the seat closer to her. "I'll tell you what it means, chicken. When on Earth, don't be a Fizbian."

*

The consul's wife, an old mauve creature, did not seem overpleased to see Tarb, since the younger, prettier Fizbian definitely took the spotlight away from her. The press had, of course, seen Tarb before, but at that time they hadn't been able to communicate directly with her and they didn't, she now found out, think nearly as much of Stet as he did of them.

Tarb couldn't attempt to deviate much from Stet's questions, for the consul's wife was not very cooperative and the consul himself watched both women narrowly. He was a good friend of Stet's, Tarb knew, and apparently Stet had taken the other man into his confidence.

When the interviews were over and the consular party had left, Tarb remained to chat with the Terrestrial journalists. Despite Griblo's worried objections, she joined them in the Moonfield Restaurant, where she daringly partook of a cup of coffee and then another and another.

After that, things weren't very clear. She dimly remembered the other reporters assuring her that she shouldn't disfigure her lovely wings with a stole . . . and then pirouetting in the air over the bar to prolonged applause . . . and then she was in the taxi again with Griblo shaking her.

"Wake up, Tarb—we're almost at the office! Stet'll have me plucked for this!"

Tarb sat up and pushed her crest out of her eyes. The sky was growing dark. They must have been gone a long time.

"I'll never hear the end of this," Griblo moaned. "Why, if only he could get someone to fill my place, Stet would fire me like a shot! Not that I wouldn't quit if I could get another job."

"Oh, it'll be mostly me he'll be mad at." Tarb pulled out her compact. Stet had warned her not to polish her eyeballs in public, but the ground with him! Her head hurt. And her feathers, she saw in the mirror, had turned almost beige. She looked horrible. She felt horrible. And Stet would probably think she was horrible.

"When Stet's mad," Griblo prophesied darkly, "he's mad at *everybody*!"

And Stet *was* mad. He was waiting in the newsroom, his emerald-blue eyes blazing as if he had not only polished but lacquered them.

"What's the idea of taking six hours to cover a simple story!" he shouted as soon as the door began to open. "Aside from the trivial matter of a deadline to be met—Griblo, *where's Tarb?* Nothing's happened to her, has it?"

"Naaah," Griblo said, unslinging his camera. "She took a short cut, only she got held up by a terrace. Snagged her umbrella on it, I believe. I heard her yelling when I was waiting for the elevator; I didn't know nice girls knew language like that. She should be up any minute now. . . . There she is."

He pointed to a window, through which the lissome form of the young feature writer could be seen, tapping on the glass in order to attract attention.

"Somebody better open it for her," the cameraman suggested. "Probably not meant to open from the outside. Not many people come in that way, I guess."

*

Open-mouthed, the whole newsroom stared at the window. Finally the Copy Editor got up and let a dripping Tarb in.

"Nearly thought I wouldn't make it," she observed, shaking herself in a flurry of wet pink feathers. The rest of the staff ducked, most of them too late. "Umbrella didn't do much good," she continued, closing it. It left a little puddle on the rug. "My wings got soaked right away." She tossed her wet crest out of her eyes. "Golly, but it's good to fly again. Haven't done it for months, but it seems like years." Her eye caught Miss Snow's. "You don't know what you're missing!"

"Tarb," Stet thundered, "you've been drinking coffee! *Griblo!*" But the cameraman had nimbly sought sanctuary in the dark-room.

"You'd better go home, Tarb." When Stet's eye tufts met across his nose, he was downright ugly, she realized. "Griblo can give me the dope and I'll write up the story myself. I can fill it out with canned copy. And you and I will discuss this situation in the morning."

"Won't go home when there's work to be done. Duty calls me." Giving a brief and quite recognizable imitation of a Terrestrial trumpet, Tarb stalked down the corridor to her office.

Drosmig looked up from his perch, to which he was still miraculously clinging at that hour. "So it got you, too? . . . Sorry . . . nice girl."

"It hasn't got me," Tarb replied, picking up a letter marked *Urgent*. "I've got it." She scanned the letter, then made hastily for Stet's office.

He sat drumming on his desk with the antique stainless steel spatula he used as a paperknife.

HELPFULLY YOURS

"Read this!" she demanded, thrusting the letter into his face. "Read this, you traitor—sacrificing our whole civilization to what's most expedient for you! Hypocrite! Cad!"

"Tarb, listen to me! I'm—"

"Read it!" She slapped the letter down in front of him. "Read it and see what you've done to us! Sure, we Fizbians keep to ourselves and so the only people who know anything about us are the ones who want to sell us brushes, while the people who want to help us don't know a damn thing about us and—"

"Oh, all right! I'll read it if you'll only keep quiet!" He turned the letter right-side up.

Johannesburg

Dear Senbot Drosmig:

I represent the Dzoglian Publishing Company, Inc., of which I know you have heard, since your paper has seen fit to give our books some of the most unjust reviews on record. However, be that as it may, I have opened an office on Earth with the laudable purpose of effecting an interchange of respective literatures, to see which Terrestrial books might most profitably be translated into Fizbian, and which of the authors on our own list might have potential appeal for the Earth reader.

Dealing with authors is, of course, a nerve-racking business and I soon found myself in dire need of mental treatment. What was my horror to find that this primitive, although charming, planet had no neurotones, no psychoscopes, not even any cerebrophones—in fact, no psychiatric machines at all! The very knowledge of this brought me several degrees closer to a breakdown.

Perhaps I should have consulted you at this juncture, but I admit I was a bit of a snob. "What sort of advice can a mere journalist give me," I thought, "that I could not give myself?" So, more for amusement than anything else, I determined to consult a native practitioner. "After all," I said to myself, "a good laugh is a step forward on the road to recovery."

Accordingly, I went to see this native fellow. They work entirely without machines, I understand, using something like witchcraft. At the same time, I thought I might pick up some material for a jolly little book on primitive customs which I could get some unknown writer to throw together inexpensively. Strong human interest items like that always have great reader-appeal.

The native chap—doctor, he calls himself—was most cordial, which he should have been at the price I was paying him. One thing I must say about these natives—backward they may be, but they have a very shrewd commercial sense. You can't even imagine the trouble I had getting those authors to sign even remotely reasonable contracts . . . which in part accounts for my mental disturbance, I suppose.

Well, anyway, I handed the native a privacy waiver carefully filled out in Terran. He took it, smiled and said, "We'll discuss this afterward. My contact lenses have disappeared; I suppose one of my patients has stolen them again. Can't see a thing without them."

So we sat down and had a bit of a chat. He seemed remarkably intelligent for a native; never interrupted me once.

"You are definitely in great trouble," he told me when I'd finished. "You need to be psycho-analyzed."

"Good, good," I said. "I see I've come to the right shop."

"Now just lie down and make yourself comfortable."

"Lie down?" I repeated, puzzled. I have an excellent command of Terran, but every now and then an idiom will throw me. "I tell the truth, sir, and when I am required by force of circumstances to lie, I lie up."

"No," he said, "not that kind of lying. You know, the kind you do at night when you go to sleep."

"Oh, I get you," I said idiomatically. Without further ado, I flung off my ulster and flew up to a thingummy hanging from the ceiling—chandelier, I believe, is the native term—flipped upside down, and hung from it by my toes. Wasn't the Presidential Perch, by any means, but it wasn't bad at all. "What do I do next?" I inquired affably.

"My dear fellow," the chap said, whipping out a notebook from the recesses of his costume, "how long have you had this delusion that you are a bird—or is it a bat?"

"Sir," I said as haughtily as my position permitted, "I am neither a bird nor a bat. I am a Fizbian. Surely you have heard of Fizbians?"

"Yes, yes, of course. They come from another country or planet or something. Frankly, politics is a bit outside my sphere. All I'm interested in is people—and Fizbians are people, aren't they?"

"Yes, certainly. If anything, it's you who. . . . Yes, they are people."

"Well, tell me then, Mr. Liznig, when was it you first started thinking you were a bat or a bird?"

I tried to control myself. "I am neither a bird nor a bat! I am a Fizbian! I have wings! See?" I fluttered them.

He peered at me. "I wish I could," he said regretfully. "Without my glasses, though, I'm as blind as a bat—or a bird."

Well, the long and the short of it is that the natives are planning to certify me as insane and incarcerate me, pending the doctor's decision as to whether my delusion is that I am a bird or a bat. They are using my privacy waiver as commitment papers.

Save me, Senbot Drosmig, for I feel that if I have to wait for the doctor's glasses to be delivered, I shall indeed go mad.

Distractedly yours,

Tgos Liznig

"I'll handle this myself," Stet said crisply. "I'll tell the consul to advise the Terran State Department that this man should be deported as an undesirable alien. That'll solve the problem neatly. We can't have this contaminating the pure stream of Terrestrial literature with—"

"But aren't you going to explain to them that he's perfectly sane?" Tarb gasped.

"No need to bother. He'll be grateful enough to get off the planet. Besides, how do I know he is perfectly sane?"

"Stet Zarnon, you're perfectly horrid!"

"And you, Tarb Morfatch, are disgustingly drunk. Now you go right home and sleep it off. I know I was too harsh with you—my fault for letting you go out alone with Griblo in the first place when you've been here only a few months. Might have known those Terran journalists would lead you astray. Nice fellows, but irresponsible." He flicked out his tongue. "There, I've apologized. Now will you go home?"

"Home!" Tarb shrieked. "Home when there's work to be done and—"

"—and you're not going to be the one to do it. Tarb," he said, attempting to seize her foot, which she pulled away, "I was going to tell you tomorrow, but you might as well know tonight. I've taken you off the column for good. I have a better job for you."

She looked at him. "A better job? Are you being sarcastic? What as?"

"As my wife." He got up and came over to her. She stood still, almost stunned. "That solves the whole problem tidily. An office is no place for you, darling—you're really a simple home-girl at heart. Newspaper work is too strenuous for you; it upsets you and makes you nervous and irritable. I want you to stay home and take care of our house and hatch our eggs—unostentatiously, of course."

"Why, you—" she spluttered.

He put his foot over her mouth. "Don't give me your answer now. You're in no condition to think. Tell me tomorrow."

*

It rained all night and continued on into the morning. Tarb's head ached, but she had to make an appearance at the office. First she vizzed an acquaintance she had made the day before; then she took her umbrella and set forth.

As she kicked open the door to the newsroom, all sound ceased. Voices stopped abruptly. Typewriters halted in mid-click. Even the roar of the presses downstairs suddenly seemed to mute. Every head turned to look at Tarb.

Humph, she thought, removing her plastic oversocks, *so suppose I was a little oblique yesterday. They needn't stare at me. They never stare at Drosmig. Just because I'm a woman, I suppose!* The gate crashed loudly behind her.

"Oh, Miss Morfatch," Miss Snow called. "Mr. Zarnon said he wanted to see you as soon as you came in. It's urgent." And she giggled.

"Really?" Tarb said. "Well, he'll just have to wait until I've wrung out my wings." Sooner or later, she would have to face Stet, but she wanted to put it off as long as possible.

She opened the door to her office and halted in amazement. For, seated on a stool behind the desk, haggard but vertical, was Senbot Drosmig, busily reading letters and blue-penciling comments on them with his feet.

"Good morning, my dear," he said, giving her a wan smile. "Surprised to see me functioning again, eh?"

"Well—yes." She opened her dripping umbrella mechanically and stood it in a corner. "How—"

"I realized last night that all that happened to you was my fault. You were my responsibility and I failed you."

"Oh, don't be melodramatic, Senbot. I wasn't your responsibility and you didn't fail me. Not that I'm not glad to see you up and doing again, but—"

"But I did fail you!" the aged journalist insisted. "And, in the same way, I failed my people. I shouldn't have given in. I should have fought Zarnon as you, my dear, tried to do. But it isn't too late!" The fire of the crusader lit up in his watery old eyes. "I can still fight him and his sacred crows—his Earthlings! If I have to, I can go over his head to Grupe. Grupe may not understand Stet's moral failings, but he certainly will comprehend his commercial ones. Grupe owns stock in other Fizbian enterprises besides the *Times*. Autofax, for example."

"Oh, Senbot!" Tarb wailed. "The whole thing's such an awful mess!"

"I don't think it'll be necessary to threaten that far," he comforted her. "Stet is no fool. He knows which side of his breadnut is peeled."

"I'm sure you'll do a wonderful job," she exclaimed, impulsively giving a ritual *entrechat*. "And I wish I could stay and help you, but. . . . "

"I know, my dear."

"You do?" She was puzzled. "But how did the news get around so quickly?"

He shrugged. "The Terrestrial grapevine is almost as efficient as the Fizbian. Didn't you notice any change in the—ah—atmosphere when you came in?"

"Oh, was that the reason?" Tarb laughed merrily. "Somehow it never occurred to me that they could have heard so soon."

"But the morning editions have been out for hours."

The door to the office was flung open. Stet stormed in, bristling with a most unloverlike rage.

"Miss Morfatch—" he waved a crumpled copy of the *Terrestrial Tribune* at her—"when I give an order, I expect to be obeyed! Didn't Miss Snow tell you to report directly to my office the instant you came in? Although that's a question I don't have to ask; I know Miss Snow, at least, is someone I can trust."

"I was coming to see you, Stet," Tarb said soothingly. "Right away."

"Oh, you were, were you? And have you seen this?" Stet fairly threw the paper at her. Smack in the middle of the front page was a picture of herself in full flight over the airfield bar. Not a very good picture, but what could you expect with Terrestrial equipment? When the autofax came, perhaps she would be done justice.

FIZBIAN NEWSHEN GIVES EARTH A FLUTTER

"Though No Mammal, I Pack a Lot of Uplift," Says Beautiful Fizbian Gal Reporter

"I feel that you Terrans and we Fizbians can get along much better," lovely Tarb Morfatch, Fizbus *Times* feature writer, told her fellow-reporters yesterday at the Moonfield Restaurant, "if we learn to understand each other's differences as well as appreciate our similarities.

"With commerce between the two planets expanding as rapidly as it has been," Miss Morfatch went on, "it becomes increasingly important that we make sure there is no clash of mores between us. Where adaptation is impossible, we must both adjust. 'When in Rome, do as the Romans do' is an outmoded concept in the complex interstellar civilization of today. The Romans must learn to accept us as we are, and vice versa.

"Forgive me if I've offended you by my frankness," she said, sticking out her tongue in the charming gesture of apology that is acquiring such a vogue on Earth, Belinda Romney and many other socialites having enthusiastically adopted it, "but you've violated our privacy so many times, I feel I'm entitled to hurt your feelings just a teeny-weeny bit. . . . "

"Those Terran journalists," Tarb said admiringly. "Never miss a trick, do they? Am I in all the other papers too, Stet? Same cheesecake?"

"You've made an ovulating circus out of us—that's what you've done!"

"Nonsense. Good strong human interest stuff; it'll make us lovable as chicks all over the planet. Gee—" she read on—"did I say all that while I was caffeinated? I ought to turn out some pretty terrific copy sober."

"And to think you, the woman I had asked to make my wife, did this to me."

"Oh, that's all right, Stet," Tarb said without looking up from the paper. "I wasn't going to accept you, anyway."

"Good for you, Tarb," Drosmig approved.

"You're going back to Fizbus on the next liner—do you hear me?" Stet raged.

She smiled sunnily. "Oh, but I'm not, Stet. I'm going to stay right here on Earth. I like it. You might say the spiritual aura got me."

He snorted. "How can you possibly stay? You don't have an independent income and this is an expensive planet. Besides, I won't let you stay on Earth. I have considerable influence, you know!"

"Poor Stet." She smiled at him again. "I'm afraid the Fizbian press—the Fizbian consul even—are pretty small pullets beside the Solar Press Syndicate. You see, I came in this morning only to resign."

He stared at her.

"Yesterday," she informed him, "I was offered another position—as feature writer for the SP. I hadn't decided whether or not to accept when

I reported back last evening, but you made up my mind for me, so I called them this morning and took the job. My work will be to explain Fizbians to Terrans and Terrans to Fizbians—as I wanted to do for the *Times*, Stet, only you wouldn't let me."

"It's no use saying anything to you about loyalty, I suppose?"

"None whatsoever," she said. "I owe the *Times* no loyalty and I'm doing what I do out of loyalty to Fizbus . . . plus, of course, a much higher salary."

"I'm glad for you, Tarb," Drosmig said sincerely.

"Be glad for yourself, Senbot, because Stet will have to let you conduct the column your way from now on. Either it'll supplement my work in the Terrestrial papers or he'll look like a fool. And you do hate looking like a fool, don't you, Stet?"

He didn't answer.

"Better give up, Stet." She turned to Drosmig. "Well, good-by, Senbot—or, rather, so long. I'm sure we'll be seeing each other again. Good-by, Stet. No hard feelings, I hope?"

He neither moved nor spoke.

"Well . . . good-by, then," she said.

The door closed. Stet stared after her. The forgotten umbrella dripped forlornly in the corner.

www.ingramcontent.com/pod-product-compliance
Lightning Source LLC
Chambersburg PA
CBHW030416310726
48979CB00002B/432

* 9 7 9 8 8 8 0 9 0 5 4 0 9 *